# Grandma Gets Grumpy

## ANNA GROSSNICKLE HINES

Clarion Books / New York

*For Michelle, Casey, Lassen, Brian, Kelly,*
*Kevin, Andy, Paul, Heather and Laura*
*and their Grandma Ruth*
*who only gets grumpy when it's absolutely necessary.*

Clarion Books
a Houghton Mifflin Company
Text and illustrations copyright © 1988 by Anna Grossnickle Hines

*Library of Congress Cataloging-in-Publication Data*
Hines, Anna Grossnickle.
Grandma gets grumpy.

Summary: Spending the night at Grandma's house, Lassen
and her cousins have fun but discover that there are
limits to Grandma's patience.
[1. Grandmothers—Fiction] I. Title.
PZ7.H572Gr 1988 [E] 87-17874
ISBN 0-89919-529-6

NI 10 9 8 7 6

Every time we go to my Grandma's house we stay all night. Mama and Papa sleep on the sofa-bed in the living room. I sleep in my sleeping bag on the floor in Grandma's room.

"Now don't snore, Lassen," Grandma says.

"I don't snore! You snore!" I say. But we are just teasing each other.

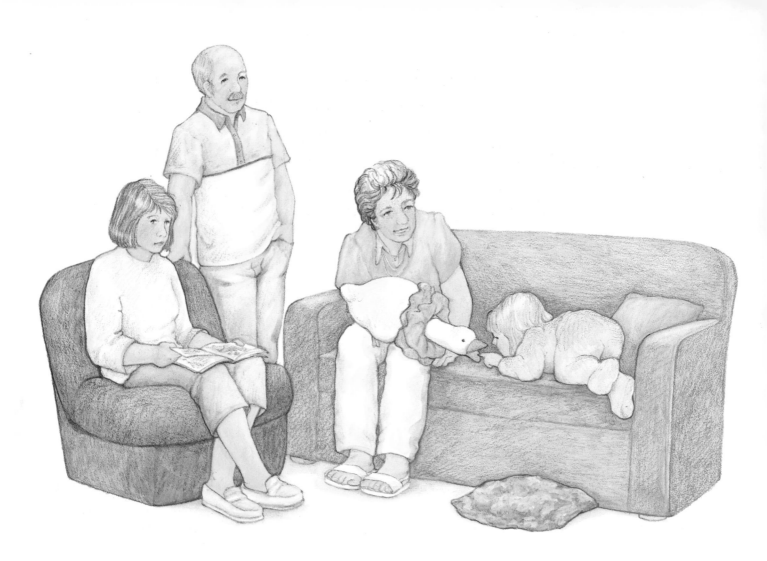

Grandma plays "go fish" with me and tickles me with her
Silly-Goose puppet.

Papa says, "Sofas are for sitting on!"

Mama says, "Stop running in the house!"

Grandma gives me hugs and says, "She just has lots of
energy, don't you, Lassen?"

Grandma has a box of toys and a whole drawer full of old clothes for playing dress-up. She likes kids.

Mama says, "Time to clean up."

Papa says, "Get ready for bed and brush your teeth."

Grandma reads me stories and gives me ice cream. I like to stay all night with Grandma.

The last time we visited Grandma, Mama and Papa went to a party at Aunt Sue and Uncle Jim's house. Grandma said they had to sleep over there because all my cousins were coming to stay with Grandma and me.

"Yippee!" I said.

"Not so loud, Lassen," said Papa.

"Are you sure you want to do this, Mom?" Mama asked.

"Don't worry," Grandma said. "We'll get along fine, won't we, Lassen?"

Aunt Sue brought Brian and Kevin. "Here they are, Mom," she said. "Are you sure you want to do this?"

"We'll be fine, won't we boys?" Grandma said. She winked at us.

Uncle Joe and Aunt Sherri brought Casey and Michelle.

Brian and Kevin and Casey and Michelle and I all hugged each other and yelled, "Hooray! Hooray!"

"Quiet down!" Uncle Joe said.

"Be good," said Mama.

"Do what Grandma tells you," said Aunt Sue.

"Are you sure you can handle all five of them, Mom?" asked Uncle Joe.

"Sure," Grandma said. "You go on and have a good time. We'll be fine."

Grandma shooed all the grown-ups out and closed the door behind them. She made hot dogs, macaroni and cheese, and green beans for dinner. We like hot dogs, macaroni and cheese, and green beans.

Then Brian and Casey and I played Chinese checkers. Kevin and Michelle made a tower of blocks. We made a bigger one. They both crashed.

We made a tower of kids. Kevin got squished 'cause he's too little. He started crying.

"Be careful," Grandma said.

We zoomed the cars under the sofa. We zoomed ourselves on top of the sofa.

"Settle down," Grandma said. "Someone might get hurt."

"Wheee!" Casey tried one more zoom. Grandma looked at him. She wasn't smiling.

We settled down.

We made roads for the cars. We made them go all over the house. Grandma doesn't care if we make a big mess. She likes kids.

I put on a beautiful dress to be a princess. Brian was the dad.
Casey was the fireman.

Michelle got run over by the fireman. I was the doctor and
fixed her up.

We made a hospital with all the blankets and chairs and pillows. Casey was the ambulance man. Brian was the nurse. Michelle and Kevin were the patients. But they wanted to be doctors, too.

"Grandma looks sick," I said. "I think she needs to go to the hospital." We took very good care of Grandma.

Michelle got in Grandma's lap and yawned a big, big yawn.
Then Kevin yawned. Then Grandma yawned. "I think it's
time to clean up," she said.

"But we're not done playing yet," we said.

"You can play again tomorrow," said Grandma. "How about
cleaning this up, then reading some stories?"

We wanted stories, but that mess was big. It was too big to
clean up.

"Let's have stories first and then clean up," I said.
"Yes! Yes! Yes!" said the other kids.
"No," Grandma said. "The mess gets picked up first."
I sat down on the floor for just one little minute.
"Lassen's not helping," Brian said.
I picked up a car. "I am too helping!" I said.
"Good," Grandma said. "We need everyone's help."

I was getting a big blanket. Casey was getting it, too. We fell down on top of each other.

Casey and I made a ghost together under the blanket and scared Kevin. Kevin jumped on the sofa. The ghost jumped on the sofa, too. Brian climbed on the sofa to save his brother.

"Oooooh," said the ghost. "Ooooooooo!!"

Kevin squealed.

"Get back, you old ghost," yelled Brian. Kevin accidentally kicked Michelle. She screamed.

"Don't hurt my sister!" Casey yelled at Kevin.
Brian pushed Casey. "You leave my little brother alone!"
Casey bumped into me. I bumped into the lamp.

"Stop!" Grandma shouted.
We didn't know she could shout.
"That is too dangerous and too noisy and
that sofa is for sitting on, not jumping on!"

We sat on the sofa. Grandma picked up her lamp.
"Grandma's getting grumpy," Casey whispered.
"She sounds just like my mom," I whispered back.
"Mine, too!" Brian said.
"And my dad," said Casey.

"You bet I do," Grandma said. We didn't know she had such good ears. "That's because I taught Lassen's mom, and Brian's mom and Casey's dad everything they know about being grumpy. And I'm older, so I've had more practice."

Grandma sat in the chair. She looked at us.

We looked at her.
"What are you going to do now," Casey said.
"I'm going to wait," Grandma said.

Grandma waited.
We waited, too.
"What are you waiting for?" Brian asked.
"I don't know," Grandma said.
We didn't know, either.

We all waited some more.
Waiting was boring. I got up and put away the blanket.

Casey put the pillows back on the sofa. Brian and Kevin picked up the dress-up clothes. Michelle picked up the cars. Grandma helped.

Casey looked at Brian and they grinned. Brian looked at me and I started to giggle. I looked at Kevin and Michelle and they laughed. Michelle looked at Grandma. Grandma laughed, too. All of us were laughing and putting things away. Grandma wasn't grumpy anymore.

Pretty soon that big mess was all cleaned up and we were
eating ice cream.

"Now it's time to brush your teeth and get into your pajamas," Grandma said.

"Oh no!" Casey said.

"We aren't tired," I started to say. But Grandma's eyebrows
went up.

We got our toothbrushes. "Watch this!" I said. I squeezed a toothpaste smile on the mirror.

"Oooh! Yeah!" said Casey. "Make the eyes!"

Brian shook his head and pointed to the doorway.

Grandma did not look happy.

I cleaned off the smile, very very carefully.

We all got our pajamas on while Grandma changed the sofa into a bed.

We climbed in and Grandma read three stories. Then she tucked us in and the Silly-Goose puppet gave us kisses. "Good night you rascals," Grandma said.

Grandma really does like kids.

And we like Grandma!